Text by John Peel

Cover Illustration by Paul Vaccarello

Interior Illustration by John Nez

Western Publishing Company, Inc.,
Racine, Wisconsin 53404

Your Briefing

Congratulations, you've been hired as a rookie detective for the Acme Detective Agency. Your goal is to outsmart Carmen Sandiego and her gang by solving the cases in this book. Each time you solve a case and make the least amount of moves you'll get a promotion.

There are four cases to solve in this book. To solve each case, start by removing the cards from the insert in the middle of this book. Divide the cards into four groups. You should have the following:

4 Bookmark / Scorecards
4 Stolen Object Cards
8 Suspect Cards
8 Map Cards

Use a different **scorecard** for each game to write down clues and eliminate suspects. Between moves use the same card as a **bookmark** to mark the place that you're in while you're investigating — sometimes you'll have to retrace your steps.

Each case involves a stolen object. Decide which case you are going to solve by picking a

stolen object card. *Put the other stolen object cards away until you are ready to solve those cases.*

*As you read each case you will be given clues about different suspects. Use those clues and the ones on the back of the **suspect cards** to decide which suspect you must capture. When you have made your decision, put the other suspect cards aside. The suspect card you have chosen serves as your warrant for their arrest.*

*Use the **map cards** for information on the various countries that you'll have to visit while tracking down a suspect. Put aside any cards that don't fit the clues you are given, until you have only one map card left.*

Each time you are told to go to a different number in the story, mark that move point on your scorecard. At the end of each game, add up the total points. Check your score on the last page to see if you've earned a promotion.

Now put on your raincoat, make sure you've got a pen or pencil, and get ready to start another Acme Detective Agency case.

Rain clouds hang over the city as you enter the Acme Detective Agency Building. It's Monday, and you know that nothing good *ever* happens on a Monday. The receptionist looks up at you and gives you a dazzling smile. You sigh because you know you've just had the one bright moment of your day.

"The Chief is waiting for you in your office," she tells you.

"It figures," you grunt. "It's Monday."

Your office is just down the hall. The bulb by the door has burned out, casting dark shadows across your nameplate. You enter the room to find the Chief sitting in your swivel chair. He looks older than he did on Friday, and you're sure his hair has turned even more gray.

"Glad you're in," he snaps. "We've got real trouble this time."

You play a hunch. "Carmen Sandiego?" you ask.

"Right," he says, and with a deep sigh he puts four folders on your desk. "She and her gang struck last night. They stole four treasures from four different countries. Take your pick where you want to start. I hope your passport's up to date."

"With Carmen and her gang on the loose, I'm always ready," you tell the Chief.

"Good," the Chief responds with just a hint of a smile. "Inside each folder are details of the stolen treasures and maps of the countries involved." Then he hands you four separate cards.

"Each time you make a move, mark down your travel points on these cards. You're in line for a promotion, and we'll be using them to grade you when the case is over."

A promotion! Maybe you'll be able to afford that new CD player, after all. Better make certain that you keep those travel points carefully noted.

Finally the Chief hands you another batch of cards. "These are snapshots of the members of Carmen's gang. Don't forget to get a warrant for the right person before you make an arrest, otherwise the thief will get away with it."

"Don't worry, Chief," you tell him. "I'm sure I'll spot the *right* clues in order to eliminate the wrong suspects. By the time I find the stolen treasures, I'll have the right robber identified, too."

"You'd better," he warns.

"Trust me, Chief."

"I do," he tells you. "You're the only one who stands a chance of catching Carmen and her gang. Well, enough talk. Decide which case you want to start on, and get going," he growls.

"Right," you call after him as he disappears through the door. You examine the four stolen object cards and follow the instructions on the one that you're going after.

If you've chosen to recapture:

- The Torch from the Statue of Liberty
   —go to 74
- The Stradivarius Violin — go to 130
- The Great Wall of China — go to 27
- The Mountain Gorilla — go to 106

THE CHASE

1. You've arrived in Wellington, the capital of New Zealand. You check your guidebook, and find that the native Maoris discovered the two main islands in the fourteenth century. The first European to discover the place was Abel Tasman, who named it Zeeland, after the Dutch province he had sailed from. You wonder what you'll discover here yourself.

Sure enough, your first discovery is the local Acme agent. He hands you a sheet of paper.

"I've found three witnesses who saw the woman you're after. I've checked all of the airlines, and there are only three outgoing flights she could have taken today. I haven't been able to narrow it down any more. Maybe you'll be able to do better."

"You did pretty good, kid," you tell him. "Acme likes bright agents like you." He grins with pride as you take the sheet and read what it says:

If you decide to check out:

The farmer — go to number 41

The librarian — go to number 169

The banker — go to number 102

☛

If you're all done investigating, and want to fly out to:
China — go to number 65
Soviet Union — go to number 80
Canada — go to number 145

2. You've arrived in Uganda, but there's no one here to meet you. You get on the phone to the local office. They don't know why you're in Uganda, either. Maybe you'd better take a trip to 18.

3. As you come closer to the kangaroo wrangler, he whips out a boomerang and throws it at you. You dive to the ground just as the boomerang whizzes over your head. Then it spins back to the wrangler. He's so amazed that he missed you, he forgets to duck. The boomerang knocks him out. You go over, and find a V.I.L.E. membership card in his pocket. You're definitely getting close now! You'd better head back to Canberra (157), fast !

4. As you arrive in India's capital city of New Delhi, the police officer is directing traffic. You ask him about the suspicious woman he saw earlier.

"Ah, I recall her," he tells you. "She was an elegant woman with brown hair."

"Did she let slip anything about where she might be going?" you ask him.

"Not a word," he says. "But I did see part of the folder that held her plane tickets. I couldn't make any words, but it looked like the ticket was in spanish."

An airline ticket in spanish. Not much to go on, but it's something. Time to head back to 170.

5. You've arrived in New York, but there are no Acme agents here. With a sinking feeling, you realize that you'd better take a trip to 18.

6. The coffee farmer greets you with a smile. He's busy sorting through red coffee beans. "Funny color for coffee," you tell him.

"Ah, the beans are always like this. It's not until we roast them that they turn brown and smell like coffee," he replies.

"Cool," you answer. "Maybe you can tell me something about the man I'm looking for?" And you show him a picture.

"Well, he said that he was going to another coffee-producing country," the farmer says. "He wore a big hat, so I didn't see much of his face. He did have blue eyes, though. Does that help you?"

"Some," you admit, making a note of what he's told you. Time to go back to San Juan (40).

7. New Zealand has lots of high mountains, so it's a great place for skiing. You find the skier you want, and she smiles when you ask her about the man you're after.

"Yes, I remember him." She laughs. "He was really silly. He kept talking to me in Spanish. Oh, and yes, he told me he was a uranium prospector. He didn't look like one, though."

These could be the clues you're after. Time to go back to Canberra and check (42).

8. You arrive in Rome, Italy, feeling that this case is about to break right open. Suddenly you spot a tour guide in the airport lobby. He's telling a bunch of camera-laden tourists about the legendary foundation of Rome in 753 B.C. by the twins Romulus and Remus. When he sees you, he stops at the part where they're adopted by a wolf, and starts to run. Thinking quickly, you throw your guidebook at his feet. He trips

over it and falls to the ground.

"Okay," you tell him angrily, slapping handcuffs on him. "Talk."

"I don't know anything," he insists, "except that I found a note in my pocket with your picture and some money. I was to stop you here."

"Which one of these people gave you my picture?" you ask, showing him three photographs.

"I'm not sure," the tour guide replies.

If you think it was:

The man from Milan — *go to 132*
Lisa from Pisa — *go to 91*
The tourist from Turin — *go to 22*

9. The factory worker is busy sewing away at a huge stack of clothing.

"How are you doing today?" you ask.

"So-so," she answers.

"Well, can you tell me anything about this woman?" you ask while showing her a photograph.

The worker pauses and thinks. "I have seen this woman. She mentioned that she was going to an island on her next flight."

You realize that you've gotten all the information you're going to get out of this factory worker. Better head back to Beijing (119).

10. You find the British bobby — that's what they call police officers in England. You think it's strange, but they're nicknamed after the founder of the police, Sir Robert Peel. You look at the bobby's odd, pointed helmet and wonder if his head is pointed underneath. You decide not to ask about his head. Instead show him a picture of the woman you're looking for.

"Yes, I remember her." He smiles. "Very pretty, she was."

"Did she say where she was going?" you ask.

"Only that she was interested in how wheat is grown," he replies. "I was more interested in her lovely long —"

"Quite," you agree. This is obviously the only useful information you'll get out of him! Time to head back to London (136) and check out what you know.

11. You get off the plane in Mecca, Saudi Arabia. The place is crowded with pilgrims visiting the holy city of Mecca. It's the birthplace of Mohammed, the prophet of the religion of Islam. Over half a million pilgrims from sixty different countries around the world visit here each year. The pilgrimage is called the *hajj*.

Despite the crowd, the local Acme man finds

you. He's obviously a good detective, if he can spot you in this crowd. But then again, you're the only one in a trench coat and fedora.

"What's the news?" you ask him.

"Your man definitely arrived here. I've managed to find three people who saw him. If you talk to them, they may be able to help you."

"Any connecting flights?" you ask.

"Three," the detective answers. "He could have left on any of them, hidden by these crowds."

"Yeah." You sigh. "Crowds are good camouflage for a crook."

If you want to interview:
The used-camel salesman — go to 76
The date trader — go to 15
The oil driller — go to 128

If you're hot on the trail, take a flight to:
Japan — go to 96
The United Kingdom — go to 160
India — go to 58

12. You get off the plane in San Juan, Puerto Rico. There's no one from the local office here, so you call in. "Are you crazy?" they tell you. "You'd better go to 18."

So — what are you waiting for?

13. This is Beijing, China. As you leave the airport terminal, a taxi driver pulls up and hands you a note. You glance at it. It tells you not to unpack your bags — but go to 18 right away.

14. You're in luck. The Bantu tribesman is a ranger at the Kidepo Valley National Park. The park is world famous and contains herds of rhinoceroses, elephants ,and giraffes.

"Can you tell me anything about this man?" You show the ranger a photograph.

"I didn't see the man," the ranger replied. "But I saw his tracks. "He's a heavy man with black hair." The tribesman grins. "He dropped his comb, and I found it."

"Any idea where he might have gone next?" you ask.

"Well, I understand it was to be an island somewhere."

You thank him for his help, and ponder your next move. Go back to Kampala (79) while you think about what you'll do next.

15. When you arrive in the marketplace, it's very crowded. Finally you spot the date trader.

"Can you tell me anything about the man I'm after?" you ask , showing her a photograph.

She smiles, very cheerfully. "Oh, yes. He asked me for a date."

"Did you sell him any?" you ask.

"No," she corrects you. "I mean, he asked me to go out with him. He offered to take me to his next port of call. He was going to go fishing."

"Sounds fishy to me," you tell her.

"Me too," she agrees. "Anyway, he left in a huff after I wouldn't go away with him."

You think over what she's told you while you head back to Mecca (11).

16. Saudi Arabia is the largest country on the Arabian peninsula. It is mostly desert, but very rich in oil.

The local agent greets you as you leave the airport terminal. "I've managed to find you three people who saw the woman you're looking for," he tells you. "And there have been only three flights out of the country today."

He hands you a list, and you look it over.

If you want to talk to:

The water diviner — go to 82

The taxi driver — go to 105

The man who makes hourglasses — go to 54

If you've discovered where your suspect has gone and decide to follow her to:

Hawaii — go to 121
Japan — go to 155
Italy — go to 8

17. You've arrived in China. As you get off the plane, you hear your name across the loudspeaker. You check in at the information desk and find a message from the Chief. It tells you to go to 18 immediately. It 's not very far, so you take the next taxi.

18. You realize that you've been fooled by Carmen's gang. There's no one here at all. You'd better hurry back to your last port of call. You did remember to leave your card in the right spot to mark your place, didn't you? And don't forget to mark the travel point for having to retrace your steps. Better luck next time.

19. The Sikh is a bearded man who wears a white turban. His name is Singh. Then you find out that all male Sikhs are named Singh. You hope you never have to use the local phone book.

"What can you tell me about the man I'm after?" you ask him.

"Only that he was reading a book about learning Spanish. He had blue eyes, but I couldn't see his hair."

"One last thing," you ask. "How come you're all called Singh?"

"It means 'lion'," he tells you. "We are all brave lions here."

Nice. Maybe you'd best not start a fight with any Sikhs! You decide to head back to New Delhi (151) to think over what you've learned.

20. You're on the trail of Kari Meback. Better head on to 86.

21. Your plane lands in the Soviet Union. You take a taxi to the capital city of Moscow and go immediately to the famous Red Square. You see the Kremlin rise in front of you as you enter the square. In Russian, *Kremlin* means a fortified area inside a city, but most people think only of Moscow's Kremlin when they hear the word. It is the site of the tomb of Lenin, the founder of the Soviet Union. The Kremlin also houses government agencies as well as museums.

You spot your contact waiting in line to see Lenin's famous glass tomb.

"Sorry about this," he tells you, "but there's such a wait to see this tomb that I couldn't risk losing my place in line."

"Well, I hope you did your work first," you tell him, hoping he'll see that you're a little annoyed.

He hands you a list. "I did indeed," he says smugly. "There are three possible contacts and three possible places that your man might have gone to." The line starts to move again and the agent is carried along. You are left holding his list. You sigh and read it.

If you want to interrogate:
The samovar salesman — go to 112
The cosmonaut — go to 38
The KGB agent — go to 57

If you want to leave for:
India — go to 151
Greenland — go to 139
China — go to 13

22. The tourist from Turin turns out to be a V.I.L.E. agent. You can tell this instantly from his shifty eyes and nervous movements.

"You're getting too close," he growls at you,

getting ready to run.

Thinking quickly, you pounce on him. In one swift move you handcuff him. Sighing with relief, you call the police to arrest the agent. Obviously, you're very close to your target now. You have to check on the other contacts, so you head back to Rome (8).

23. You arrive in the Soviet Union. The contact you're expecting isn't at the airport. Instead, a KGB agent comes up and hands you a message telling you to go to 18 — right away!

24. Your contact is working outside the New York Public Library. He's a pretty good mime, climbing in and out of invisible boxes and riding invisible bicycles. When he collects his coins from the passersby, you talk to him.

"I hear you may be able to tell me something."

He shakes his head and points to his mouth.

Of course! He's a mime. He never says a word. You sigh. This isn't going to be an easy case. "Okay," you agree. "What can you show me?"

The mime smiles, then runs around with his arms out. "Airplane," you guess, and he nods. "But where to?" you ask. He points uptown. "Times Square?" you guess. He shakes his head and points again. This time he shudders.

"Somewhere scary?" you ask.

Wrong again. The mime makes gestures of pulling on a coat. "Somewhere cold," you realize. He nods, and shakes your hand. So now you know your man is heading north to somewhere cold. Better check to see what else you can discover. You're hoping the next contact can talk! You head back to the airport (74).

25. You arrive in San Juan, Puerto Rico. As you get off the plane, a smiling girl hands you an envelope. There's a card in it. Funny, it's not your birthday. You open it, and read the verse:

Roses are red, violets are blue,

Boy, have I made a sucker out of you.

You've certainly come to just the wrong place,

So head for 18, and you'd better make haste!

26. You've arrived with a warrant to arrest Kari Meback. She's not here right now, so you'd better head for 86.

27. As you get off the plane in Beijing, you remember that this capital of China was once known as Peking. In fact, Beijing is a number of cities. There's the Outer City, built during

the famous Ming Dynasty of the sixteenth century. North of this is the older Inner City, a square with almost fifteen miles of walls around it. Inside this is the Imperial City, and right in the middle of this is the Forbidden City, which contains all the imperial palaces and was once forbidden to any commoner. Nowadays, though, the Forbidden City is a museum open to all.

This case seems to have a lot of walls around it! Suddenly, a young woman from the Acme office here approaches you and bows. You bow back politely.

"Welcome to China," she says and offers you a sheet of rice paper. On it, in a beautiful, neat script, you read the following:

Three informants have been found. If you wish to talk to:

The museum guard — go to 32
The tea picker and packer — go to 81
The chess player — go to 107

The suspect may have gone to:
The United States — go to 63
Saudi Arabia — go to 135
Puerto Rico — go to 12

28. You wonder what *no actor* might be. As

you arrive at the theater, you see the stage manager. "I'm looking for no actor," you tell him.

"Then who are you looking for?" he asks. "A writer, a stagehand, or someone else?" You show him the list, and he laughs. "Ah, not no actor, *Noh* actor," he says. You start to wonder if he's crazy, or if you are. He explains, "The classic drama of Japan is called Noh. It uses poetry, dance, and song, to tell stories that date back as far as the fourteenth century."

"Oh. Noh," you say. "I see."

Thankfully, the actor you're looking for arrives. You ask him to tell you what he knows.

"I saw the man you're after," he tells you. "He had gray eyes and was trying to find a theater showing Godzilla movies. I told him he was in the wrong place. He then said he was heading off to look for gold."

You thank the actor and the stage manager and decide to head back to Tokyo (96) and think about what to do next.

29. You've arrived in New York City. There's a heat wave going on, and everyone seems to be grouchy. You can't find your contact so you decide to call the local office. The person on the phone is annoyed. "Why are you here?" he asks.

"You should be at 18 — now!"

30. It's New York City, but it's two in the morning. The place seems deserted. You ask at the hotel information desk about your contact, but you're told there's no one here. There is, however, another plane ticket for you. It's for 18, so you head on out again.

31. You've got a warrant to arrest Carmen Sandiego herself — but you should have known better. She's slipped through your fingers again. You'd better head for 86.

32. China has a long history that stretches back to 5000 B.C. There are lots of museums all over the country, with plenty of fascinating relics to see. Your orders are to go to the local museum and contact the museum guard. Trouble is, which museum? When you finally find the right museum, you run up to the guard at the door.

"I understand that you saw the woman I'm after," you say, trying to catch your breath.

"That's right," he agrees. "She was acting very suspiciously. I think she was trying to steal a priceless Ming vase. When I went over to investigate, she ran out quickly. I didn't 👉

get a chance to see what she looked like, but she did drop this."

It's a book called *Teach Yourself Oil Drilling*. Great! It has to contain a clue about where your thief might be going next. You go back to 27 to check out your options.

33. The used-lei salesman turns out to be a plant. The lei is a traditional flower garland that is a symbol of peace, but this salesman is trying to strangle you with one!

You're not so easily caught, though. You kick him in his shin, and while he hops around in pain, you land a good right hook to his jaw. He's lei'ed out cold. If this is a V.I.L.E. henchman, then you've got to be close! Back to the airport, fast (123)!

34. The snake charmer is playing a tune on

his flute as you arrive. A deadly cobra in a basket is dancing in time to the music. The man stops playing. "Do you like the snake?" he asks.

"It's charming," you reply. "But maybe you can tell me something about the man I'm looking for. He's a bigger snake than the one in your basket."

"Indeed I can," the performer tells you. "He didn't like my snake at all. Said it reminded him of too many people he knew. Then he said he was going to an island next. He said that he hoped there weren't any snakes there. He was a funny person. I never heard of someone not liking snakes. *You* like snakes, don't you?"

"Love them," you assure him.

"Want to play with mine?" he offers.

"Uh, some other time," you reply. "I'm in a hurry to get back to the airport (151)."

35. As you get off the plane in Ottawa, you're approached on the runway by a member of the Royal Canadian Mounted police. These famous lawmen are dressed in distinctive red coats, so you can spot him instantly. He doesn't look happy, however.

"Boy, are you in the wrong place," he shouts to you. "You should be at 18." You call out thanks as you head for the ticket counter.

36. Well, you've got your warrant to arrest Luke Warmwater, but he's nowhere to be found. With a sinking feeling, you head for 86.

37. When the lumberjack sees you, he stops chopping down one of the huge trees he's working on. He leans on his immense ax as you ask about the woman you're after.

"Oh, sure, I saw her," he tells you. "Couldn't miss her. She had bright red hair. She said she was going to go drilling for oil."

You thank him for his help and head back to the airport (145). As you leave, you hear his axe thudding into the tree behind you. You're glad you don't have to do all that work!

38. The cosmonaut is the Soviet version of an astronaut. He's in training at Star City, not far from Moscow, where the Soviets launch their space missions. Your contact takes time off from his training to talk with you.

"I recall the man you're after," the cosmonaut tells you. "He had shifty blue eyes. He told me he always wanted to see how rice was grown, because he loves rice pudding. I told him that we don't have rice plants 👈

here in Star City, and he said that they did have them where he was going."

A clue! You head back to the airport to check everything out (21).

39. You've arrived in Wellington, New Zealand, and you discover that this is a bad move. There's no one here, so you head back to 18.

40. The Commonwealth of Puerto Rico is not actually a country. It's a self-governing part of the United States. Puerto Ricans are United States citizens. In fact, you discover as you leaf through your guidebook, Puerto Rico is Spanish for "rich port," and the island was discovered by Columbus on his second journey to the New World, in 1493.

Your contact arrives. She's a tour guide. "I've found three people who saw the man you're after. There are three places that the thief could have escaped to. I've written them down for you."

You thank her, and look at her list.
If you want to question:
The man from San Juan — go to 64

The pepper picker — go to 109 ☞

The coffee farmer — go to 6

If you want to travel to:
Saudi Arabia — go to 118
Hawaii — go to 53
Uganda — go to 79

41. In New Zealand, many of the big farms are located on rich, hilly grasslands. Farmers use trained dogs to round up and control their sheep. The farmer you've just come to see is no exception. You watch in amazement as he calls his dogs just by whistling. When the sheep are safely penned, you ask the farmer about the woman you're tracking.

"I remember her," says the farmer. "She scared my dogs, that one. I told her to clear off. She was very annoyed and said she was going after quieter animals. She was carrying a fishing rod."

"Carmen's gang can be pretty ugly," you agree.

"You can say that again," the farmer answers. You decide not to say it again and head back to the airport (1).

42. You've arrived safely in Wellington, New

Zealand. About a quarter of a million native Maori people live here. The Maoris were originally from the Pacific Islands, and settled in the islands of New Zealand in the fourteenth century. When the British began colonizing New Zealand in 1840, war broke out between the British and Maoris, and it continued for thirty years. You're glad those days are long gone.

Your local contact meets you and tells you that he's found three people who saw the man you're chasing. He also mentions that there have been three flights out of the country, but he hasn't had time to check them out yet. You take his information and examine it.

If you want to talk to:
The skier — *go to 7*
The Maori warrior — *go to 111*
The fisherman — *go to 84*

If you're ready to travel:
To the United States — *go to 168*
To the Soviet Union — *go to 23*
To Argentina — *go to 142*

43. The businessman is dressed in a dark suit, with a rolled-up umbrella and a bowler hat. He looks at your trench coat and fedora

and sniffs. "Ahh, an American," he comments. "They still don't teach you how to dress over there?"

You growl back. "We prefer to keep things casual." You decide to get right to the point with this guy. "I understand you saw the woman I'm looking for."

"Yes, by heavens, I did!" he exclaims. "Now, *she* was someone who knew how to dress! A delightful lady with heavenly blue eyes."

"Good clothes or not, she's a crook, through and through," you tell him. "Did she say where she was going?"

"Well, she did mention something about seeing an Indian. But I don't think she was aiming to go to America. She seemed too sensible for that."

"Stuck-up little drip," you mutter as you leave.

"Scarecrow!" he calls after you as you hurry back to the airport (136).

44. You find Alaska a bit of a disappointment. The Eskimo you've come to see lives in a beautiful stone house, instead of an igloo, as you had hoped. When you mention this, he laughs. "Igloos are old-fashioned," he tells you.

Oh, well. You ask him about your suspect.

"Yes, I saw him," the Eskimo answers. "He had brown hair. He told me he was looking for greener pastures, and then left. I have no idea where he went."

The Eskimo's clues aren't much help, but they're better than nothing. You head back to Godthaab to think things over (68).

45. The opera singer is practicing when you arrive. When she stops singing, you go onstage to talk to her. She begins to tell you about the classic Italian operas she's sung in, written by people like Verdi, Rossini, and Donizetti. Opera's not your thing, so you steer her back to the subject you're most interested in — the crook you're tracking down.

"He was much more interested in opera than you are," she tells you. "And he said he was a student of ballet, too."

"Never heard of him," you reply.

"Ballet is a dance style," she tells you.

"Is it like disco?" you ask. She just sighs.

"Any idea where he might have gone?" you ask.

"He mentioned going someplace where there was a lot of farmland," she answers, gruffly.

"Thanks for the clue," you answer with a smile. Time to head back to the airport (130).

46. You were dead right! The villainess behind the theft was none other than Carmen Sandiego herself. You find her tanning on the beach at Waikiki. You throw her a towel.

She catches the towel and suddenly dashes into the ocean. You expected this. Right on cue, members of the Hawaiian police force stand up on their surfboards and surround Carmen.

"I've got you covered, Carmen," you tell her. "Better give yourself up."

"You win, this time," she says with a sigh. "But next time — watch out!"

When the police take her away, you call the Chief to tell him that you've captured Carmen.

"Excellent work!" he tells you. "I'm sure you're going to get that promotion now!"

47. You arrive at the roadside stall of the newspaper vendor. "I'm looking for news," you tell him.

He gestures at the large display of papers. "I got lots," he responds.

"Do you have any news about the woman who stole the Great Wall of China?" you ask.

"Yeah, I've seen her," he says. "She bought a paper. Then she said she was going somewhere where it was legal to make steal. Didn't make any sense to me."

But it does to you. "She didn't mean *steal*," you tell him. "She meant *steel*. As in iron and steel." You both have a good laugh. Then you make your way back to the airport (63).

48. When you arrive at the library, you find a librarian who can help you. She is binding wood and bamboo strips together with thin string. "Funny-looking books," you say.

She smiles. "These are replicas of some of the oldest books in the world," she explains. "My ancestors made books like this over three thousand years ago."

You look at the strips again and shrug. "Speaking of knowledge, maybe you can give me some information about this woman." You show the librarian a picture.

"She was here," the librarian tells you. "She was asking about a country where she might buy pure wool to make sweaters."

You think about this as you head back to the airport (119). You also think how glad you are that the Chinese later invented printing on paper. It would get pretty heavy to carry about books made from wooden slats on your trips!

49. You've arrived in New York, but you

don't see your local contact. You call the office.

"What are you doing in New York?" the operator asks you. "Go to 18 right away."

50. As you deduced, the criminal you're after is none other than Justin Case! You surprise him in his hotel room, trying to play the stolen Stradivarius violin. He's not very good at it — he's trying to play rock 'n' roll!

"I want a lawyer!" he starts yelling, and then suddenly stops. "Wait a minute, *I am* a lawyer."

"Better come quietly," you tell him, while putting the treasured violin in its case.

Soon the local police arrive to arrest him. When they take him away, you call the Chief, to let him know that you've solved the case.

"Good work," he tells you. "Acme is proud of you. Now add up those travel points, and head for the back of the book. I'm sure you've earned yourself a promotion and a raise!"

51. You arrive at the local railway station with a warrant to arrest Luke Warmwater. Unfortunately, he's not the villain behind this theft. You really feel foolish. On top of all this, you have to add on another trip. Go to 86.

52. Your plane touches down in Buenos

Aires, Argentina. The country is the second largest in South America and makes up almost all of the southern part of the continent.

You read in your guidebook that it was settled by the Spanish in the seventeenth century. You also read that it is the home of the largest rodent in the world, the capybara. Great — a huge rat. "I hate rats," you mutter.

The girl from the local Acme office arrives and greets you. "I've found some people who saw the woman you're after," she tells you. "And there were three flights out of the country just before you arrived. I know she bought a ticket for one of them, but she also had two look-alikes buy tickets for the other two countries, I'm afraid."

"I'll figure it out," you tell her. "That's what I'm paid to do." You study her list.

If you want to interview:

The gaucho — go to 73

Patagonian Pete — go to 61

The fisherman — go to 166

If you're done, you can fly to:

The United States — go to 5

Puerto Rico — go to 144

Hawaii — go to 123

53. You've arrived in Hawaii. It's a beautiful

paradise of beaches, sun, and surfing. Unfortunately, you can't stay long. There's a note for you requesting that you head straight back to 18.

54. You find the hourglass maker at the edge of the desert. He has hundreds of unfilled hourglasses around him, and he's carefully measuring sand to pour into each one.

"Do you have the time to talk to me?" you ask.

He spreads his hands. "Time I have in plenty," he says with a smile.

"I'm looking for a woman who may be traveling with a stolen gorilla."

"I have seen her," he admits. "She had bewitching brown eyes."

"Did she say where she was going?"

"Only that she'd seen enough sand, and she was longing for some nice fresh fruit."

You can understand her feelings. You've also had your fill of sand. You leave the man filling the hourglasses and head back to the airport (16).

55. You're out in the wilds of Patagonia now, with a warrant to arrest Ernest Endeavor. He's not the right person. So head for 86 right now.

56. The tour guide at the volcano explodes

in anger, when you approach him. He looks at you and realizes he's not going to win. You frisk him, and find what you're looking for — a list Carmen's gang and their hideouts. The thief you're after is one of the people on this list! If you think it's:

Kari Meback — go to 20
Chuck Roast — go to 100
Carmen Sandiego — go to 46
Justin Case — go to 88
Ernest Endeavor — go to 114
Luke Warmwater — go to 51
"Auntie" Bellum— go to 163
Claire d'Loon — go to 140

57. The KGB agent is hiding in the shadows of the Kremlin. He hisses, and you go over. "I hear you're searching for the blue-eyed man who stole the Stradivarius violin from Rome," he says.

"You hear pretty well," you tell him. "You hear anything about the man?"

"Yes. I heard he bought rupees on the black market."

You thank him, and he melts away into the dark shadows. But he's given you a hot tip about where your prey may be hiding out. You go back to the airport to check it out (21).

58. You've arrived in India, and there's a holy man waiting to see you.

"I have a message for you," he says.

"From God?" you ask.

"No — from Acme. You're in the wrong place. Better head for 18."

59. You've arrived in the United States again. As you hunt around for your contact, someone bumps into you. You think it might be a pickpocket, but the mysterious person slips you a note instead. You read it and head straight for 18.

60. So this is Ottawa! Looks pretty deserted to you. You ask at your hotel desk if there are any messages for you. The desk clerk smiles and hands you a message.

"You idiot," it reads. "You should be at 18."

61. Patagonia is a huge area right down south in South America. There aren't many people around, but there are plenty of sheep. It takes you a while to cross the grasslands to find your contact, Pete. When you find him, you ask about the woman you're after.

"Ah, I recall her well!" he tells you. "She was

looking for someone who could change her money into American dollars."

You head back to the airport (52), in hopes of finding out where she might be heading.

62. You're in Japan, home of Godzilla. But no suspects. Go to 18 now.

63. You're in New York City. You love being here, in the historic five boroughs of the largest city in the United States. — Manhattan, the Bronx, Brooklyn, Queens, and Staten Island. You read in your guidebook that it was the capital of the United States from 1785 to 1790. It may not be the capital anymore, but it's still a great city to be in.

You meet your contact here, and he hands you a list. "The woman you're after talked to these people," he tells you. "And she left for one of these three places. See you around." You examine the list.

If you want to talk to:
The Wall Street broker — go to 122
The newspaper vendor — go to 47
The carriage driver — go to 92

If you want to fly to:
China — go to 17

40

The United Kingdom — go to 136
Italy — go to 154

64. You find your contact on San Juan Hill. He's a history buff, and tells you that it was here in 1898 that Theodore Roosevelt and his Rough Riders won a decisive battle in the Spanish-American War. That's all very interesting, but not what you're here for.

"Have you seen the man I'm after?" you want to know.

"Yes," the historian says. "He mentioned he was going to search for copper."

Right! You leave your contact to trace the path of the Rough Riders up the hill. You're heading back to the airport (40), hot on a fresher trail!

65. You've now arrived in China, but it might as well be the moon. There's no one here to meet you, and just a plane ticket that will take you right to 18.

66. You've arrived in the museum with a warrant to arrest Auntie Bellum. Too bad — she isn't here. Why don't you head for 86 instead?

67. Blow me down, sport! Here you are in

Australia, and it's you that's upside down! You've got a warrant to arrest Claire d'Loon, but there's no sight of her here. Better go to 86.

68. As you climb out of the aircraft, you pull your coat around you for warmth. You're in Godthaab, Greenland, now also known as Nuuk. It's bitterly cold here, which isn't too surprising, since over 80 percent of the country is permanently covered by a sheet of ice.

Your contact arrives, and you ask him, "Why on earth is this place called Greenland? Wouldn't Snowland be more appropriate?"

"Probably," he agrees. "But when Eric the Red discovered the land in 982 A.D., he called it Greenland to get people to come and settle here. Sort of a cheerful advertising campaign."

"Well, I'm glad someone can be cheerful about this cold," you answer. "So, got any hot tips for me?"

"A few," he answers. "I've found some people who saw the man you're after. And there have been three flights out since he arrived."

If you want to talk to:

The Eskimo — go to 44

The fisherman — go to 143

The farmer — go to 41

If you're ready to leave, then head for:

Saudi Arabia — go to 11
Italy — go to 159
China — go to 71

69. You arrive at the bank and spot the teller you're looking for. You decide it's time to make a quick withdrawal. When the teller reaches for your withdrawal slip you handcuff him to the window bars.

"Okay," you say to the teller, "tell me what you know."

"Someone hired me to stop you, but you didn't even give me a chance." he says with a miserable whine, as the police arrive to arrest him.

Clearly, you're getting close. You head back to the airport (142), to try another informant.

70. Crocodile Humphrey is sitting by his pool, feeding his toothy pets when you arrive.

"I've been waiting for you, snoop," he snarls. "And I think it's time you got what's coming to you?"

"Don't I even get a last meal?" you ask, thinking fast.

"You are the last meal," He laughs. "For the crocodiles."

You pull a bottle from your pocket, but it's

not pills — it's a smoke bomb. You drop it on the ground and dive for cover. Humphrey is overcome by smoke and collapses in his chair.

You take this opportunity to go through his pockets. You find a list of the hideouts for the members of the gang. Success! Your suspect is one of these. If it's:

Luke Warmwater — *go to 129*
Kari Meback — *go to 26*
"Auntie" Bellum — *go to 94*
Chuck Roast — *go to 115*
Claire d'Loon — *go to 67*
Ernest Endeavor — *go to 146*
Carmen Sandiego — *go to 165*
Justin Case — *go to 50*

71. You've arrived in China, and there's a girl waiting at the airport desk for you. She hands you a ticket. "Better leave right away," she tells you. It's for 18.

72. You're on the tiny main island of Tierra del Fuego, just off the southern coast of Argentina. You have a warrant to arrest Luke Warmwater. But there's no one in sight. Better head off to 86.

73. The gaucho is a kind of South American

cowboy. Seated on his horse, he is dressed ornately and sports a large hat on his head. He waves this (the hat, not his head) as he sees you coming.

"So," he says politely, "how may I help you?"

"Maybe you can tell me about the woman I'm after," you say, showing him her picture.

"Ah, I remember her well." He smiles. "A true beauty, that one. She said she was going somewhere where there was no industry but plenty of places to laze in the sun."

You think you know where your suspect has gone. But first you decide to head back to the airport (52) to verify your suspicions.

74. You've arrived in New York City, home of the Statue of Liberty and its stolen torch. You head down to Battery Park to take a ferry to the Statue.

As you ride through the harbor, you pass several islands. One famous island is Ellis Island. Between 1891 and 1954, twenty million immigrants passed through the island's buildings on their way to make a new home in the United States. Now the buildings have been converted into a Museum of Immigration.

Just past Ellis Island is Liberty Island, where the Statue of Liberty stands. Once you're on Liberty Island, you speak to the park ranger in charge. Luckily for you, he has a few leads.

"Three people saw the theft," the ranger admits, handing you a list. "And before we could seal off the airport, there were three flights out of here."

If you want to interrogate:
The taxi driver — go to 161
The street mime — go to 24
The pretzel seller — go to 148

If you're ready to go to:
Canada — go to 35
Hawaii — go to 120
Greenland — go to 68

75. You've arrived in New Zealand, and there's no one in sight. The place is completely empty. Suspicious of funny business, you head for the desk. Taped to the telephone is a message for you from the Chief.

"You numbskull," it reads. "Go straight to 18."

76. You find the used-camel salesman at his stall in the marketplace. As you approach he gives you a big grin and shouts, "Have I got a bargain for you! A great camel, used only by a

little old lady to go to the mosque at the —"

"I'm not here to buy a camel," you tell him. His face falls. "I'm after a little information. I'm looking for a man. One of Carmen Sandiego's gang."

"I remember him well," the trader replies. "He tried to steal one of my camels! I chased him away."

"Do you have any idea where he went?" you ask.

"He said something about an island," the salesman answers. He looks at you again. "You sure you don't want to buy a camel?"

"I'm heading back to the airport, and I don't think they allow camels as carry-on luggage."

"I'll check!" he calls, rushing after you. Instead, you make a dash back to Riyadh (11).

77. You find the cattle herder in his village, watching his small herd of cows. He greets you kindly as you approach. You show him a photograph of a woman.

"I saw her," he tells you. "She mentioned going to one of the oldest cilvilizations in the world."

You thank him and head back to the airport to check out this information (106).

78. You arrive in the famous Teatro dell'Opera,

one of the finest concert halls in Rome. Naturally, you find Claire d'Loon inside the hall, onstage. The gorilla is with her. She is trying to teach him to play the piano.

"The gig's up," you tell her.

Claire sits back from the piano and sighs. "I can't get this gorilla to play anything. I did so want a partner for my next series of piano recitals."

"I'm sure you'll find a piano partner in prison," you tell her. "Maybe you'll get lucky — you might be sent to Sing Sing."

The police take her away and you call the Chief to tell him that you've recovered the stolen gorilla and captured Claire d'Loon.

"Well done," he growls. "Better head off to the score chart at the back of the book and see if you've got that promotion!"

79. You've arrived at Kampala, the capital of Uganda. Uganda has some of the most spectacular scenery in the world. There's Lake Victoria, the source of the Nile River, which many explorers went looking for in the nineteenth century. And there's the Great Rift Valley, where fossils from ancient relatives of the human race were discovered.

But alas, you're here to discover only one thing

— the location of the thief who stole the Stradivarius violin!

Your local contact is a Baganda tribesman. He hands you a list. "I've narrowed down your search. Three people saw the thief, and there have been three flights out of here."

If you want to talk to:
The Bantu tribesman — go to 14
The park ranger — go to 83
The banana picker — go to 101

If you're ready to leave for:
Canada — go to 60
Australia — go to 157
New Zealand — go to 39

80. You've arrived safely in the Soviet Union, but it's a cold, cold day. Shivering, you approach the airline desk and ask if there's a message for you. There is. Go to 18.

81. The tea picker is working hard. You watch with fascination as she quickly pulls the best tea leaves off their bushes. Seeing your interest, she smiles at you.

"Tea is one of the oldest drinks in the world," she says. "The Chinese have been drinking it since early times. It wasn't until the seventeenth century that the Dutch introduced it to Europe."

"I love tea," you tell her. "There's nothing like a cup of tea with breakfast. And iced tea in the summer . . . ah, well! Down to business. I think you've seen the woman I'm looking for."

"Yes, she stopped by for a cup of tea," the picker answers. "She said she had a long trip ahead of her, and that where she was going, they grew corn, not tea." You thank her for her help and head back to the airport (27).

82. You find the water diviner walking along with a forked stick. Puzzled, you watch him for a while. Seeing your expression, he laughs.

"Out here in the desert, water is the most valuable thing you can find. There are thousands of oil wells in this country, but precious little water."

"Well, I'm not looking for oil or water," you tell him. "I'm after a woman who stole a gorilla."

"Ah, the brown-eyed one." He smiles. "I saw her. She said she was going to a place where they grow delicious grapes."

You thank the diviner for his help and head back to 16.

83. Uganda has lots of parks full of wonderful animals. But they have serious problems with

poachers — hunters who kill animals for their skins and tusks. So there are park rangers to keep their eyes on whoever comes in and out of the parks. That's good news for you, because one ranger saw the man you're after.

"Yes, he was here," the ranger says. "A black-haired man, right? He looked pretty suspicious to me, so I threw him out. He was very annoyed, and said he was going somewhere to look for diamonds."

You head back to the airport (79) as you think about this clue.

84. You spot the fisherman knee-deep in a beautiful clear river. When you get closer he greets you and asks, "What are you fishing for?"

"Information," you tell him. "But I'm just trying to catch a thief, not a fish."

"Yes, I saw this man," the fisherman says after looking at a picture you hand him. "He was creating a disturbance and scaring the fish, so I chased him away."

"Did he say where he was going?" you ask.

"Well, he did mumble something about south of the equator," the fisherman answers.

Hmm, time to go back to the airport (42).

85. You've got a warrant to arrest Carmen Sandiego, but when you arrive at the Coliseum, she isn't there. Instead, you find a note:

"Fooled you, you little snooper! Your trail's gone cold. Better head for 86 right away."

Don't forget to add your travel point.

86. You've tracked the thief to the right place, but you've added up the clues incorrectly. Your warrant is for the wrong person. Because you've identified the wrong thief, add ten extra travel points onto your score.

Better luck on your next case. Right now head for the score chart at the back of the book and see how you've done.

87. You've arrived in the United Kingdom, which is one country made up of England, Scotland, Wales, and Northern Ireland.

Pity there's no one here to show you around. Head back to 18.

88. You are in Hawaii, but you're stranded on the beach. Your warrant to arrest Justin Case isn't any good. That's right, he's not here. You'd better take a short trip to 86.

89. You find the wine presser hard at work in his vineyard. You expected to see him stomping

the grapes down in a big barrel, but he's using a special machine instead. He laughs when you ask why he's not jumping on the grapes.

"No one does that anymore," he tells you. "These machines work better than feet. Why, Italian grape-crushing machines are famous all over the world. A lot of wineries back in your United States buy our machines to do the crushing for them."

"Well, maybe you can do something else for me," you say. "I'm looking for this thief."

"Ah, I saw that man," the wine presser tells you, angrily. "He tried to steal a bottle of my best red wine! I threw him out. He said he was going to head for some rubles, not troubles."

You ponder this information while you head back to the airport (130).

90. So this is Argentina! You're excited as you get off the plane. The excitement is short-lived, though, as a messenger approaches you with a note from the Chief. It reads:

"Why are you here? Go immediately to 18."

91. You finally track down Lisa in Pisa. She's leaning on the Leaning Tower. As you approach, she starts climbing the tower. She's either a V.I.L.E. agent, or she hates tourists.

Fortunately, it's against the law to climb the tower of Pisa. Two policemen rush over, and they arrest her.

As they take her away, you search her handbag. You find a bottle of poison and a hand grenade in her bag. So she was ready for you. Suddenly you find a list underneath the weapons, and it tells you where all the possible suspects are hiding out. If you think it was:

    Luke Warmwater — *go to 36*
    Carmen Sandiego — *go to 85*
    Ernest Endeavor — *go to 116*
    Claire d'Loon — *go to 78*
    Justin Case — *go to 127*
    "Auntie" Bellum — *go to 66*
    Chuck Roast — *go to 158*
    Kari Meback — *go to 98*

92. You arrive at the south side of Central Park. There is a line of horse-drawn carriages

ready to take the tourists around. You find the carriage you're looking for, and feed the horse a lump of sugar. You turn to the driver and ask, "Have you've seen this woman." You show the driver a photograph.

"Yeah, I've seen her. She said she always wanted to ride around the park, so I took her. After the ride was over, she asked where the nearest bank was. She said she wanted to change her dollars into pounds."

A clue! You head back to the airport (63) to check it out.

93. Well, here you are with a warrant to arrest Justin Case, but there's no sign of the villain anywhere. There's only one thing that you can do — go straight to 86.

94. You've arrived at the Great Barrier Reef, one of the natural wonders of the world. But, wonder of wonders, there's no sign of Auntie Bellum. Your warrant isn't much use, so you'd better head for 86.

95. You find the bank you're looking for, and talk to the manager. He remembers seeing the woman you're after. "She was in here to change her shillings to yuans," he explains.

You decide that maybe you'd better do the same, and then head back to the airport (106).

96. When you get off the plane, you realize that Japan is very crowded. It consists of four main islands — Honshu, Hokkaido, Kyushu, and Shikoku — and hundreds of smaller ones.

Many of the houses are made from reinforced paper, because Japan is very volcanic and there are lots of earthquakes. The paper houses can withstand the earthquakes better. The most famous volcano, Mount Fuji, is now dormant. You're glad of that, since it's just outside of Tokyo, and you're not too far from there now!

You meet the local agent. She's done her work all right. She smiles and hands you a report. Good. It's brief:

There are three people who saw the man you're after, and three planes he could have taken to leave the country again.

If you want to speak with:

The Japanese Noh actor — go to 28
The bonsai bush man — go to 113
The sumo wrestler — go to 138

If you want to fly to:
Uganda — go to 2   ☞

New Zealand — go to 42
Puerto Rico — go to 152

97. Yukon Tom lives high in the mountains, where he prospects for gold. The Klondike gold rush at the end of the nineteenth century didn't leave much behind, but Yukon Tom's convinced he'll strike it rich one day. He grins at you as you approach his camp.

"You looking for gold?" he asks.

"No, I'm looking for a gorilla," you answer.

"Not many up here," he says. "Maybe you should be in Africa."

"The gorilla I'm looking for has been stolen. I think you might have seen the woman who took him."

"Matter of fact, I did," he replies. "She tried to steal my gold. She sure could sweet-talk, but I never did trust a woman with red hair. I kicked her out of my camp."

"Any idea where she went?"

He scratches his head. "I'm not too good at geography," he admits. "But she mentioned going someplace sunny."

You thank him and set off for Ottawa (145), while he goes back to his digging.

98. You arrive in Venice, famous for its canals. Like them, you're all wet, too. Kari Meback isn't

here, and your warrant's no good. Better head for 86.

99. The farmer has a small plot of land near Godhavn on the west coast. It's so cold, you wonder how anything ever grows here. Still, the farmer greets you politely, and you ask him about the man you're after.

"Oh, I remember him," he tells you. "He hated it here because of the cold. He said he was going to go to a warmer place, but first he had to change his money to riyals."

You say goodbye and head back to the airport (68). Good, the next place is warmer.

100. You're on Molokai, one of the smaller Hawaiian islands — and a very quiet one. In fact, there's absolutely no sign at all of the person you're here to arrest, Chuck Roast. You'd better head off to 86 to see why.

101. Bananas are a big crop in Uganda, and there are lots of banana pickers getting them ready for market. You find the man you're looking for, and ask him about the thief you're tracking down.

"Yes, he was here," the picker points out. "He had black hair. I caught him stealing some of my bananas, and chased him out."

"Any idea where he went?" you ask.

"Nope," the picker replies. "But I hope he never comes back here."

What a bummer! You head back to the airport (79) to see if you can find more clues.

102. The banker is a friendly fellow. He remembers the woman you're looking for.

"A strange lady. She was with the ugliest man I've ever seen."

"That wasn't a man," you tell him. "That was a gorilla."

"Oh. I *thought* he needed a shave," the banker replies.

"Do you have any idea where they went?" you ask him.

"Certainly," he says. "To a teller's window."

You sigh. "I meant *after* they left here." *(This banker is not the brightest man you've ever met.)*

"I heard her say they were leaving for a very *big* country," he tells you. You decide not to bank on any more answers from this banker, and head straight to the airport (1).

103. You arrive at one of the famous meat-packing ranches of Argentina. Just as you

expected, you find Chuck Roast here, watching them prepare the cattle.

You sneak up behind him and slip handcuffs on him. He almost has a heart attack when he realizes he's been caught.

"I'm looking for the torch of the Statue of Liberty. Care to throw a light on the mystery?"

"All right." He sighs. "I'll give it back."

The police take Chuck away. You collect the torch and give the Chief a call.

"I've caught Chuck Roast," you say, "and I'm sending the torch to New York City by special police."

"Great work," says the Chief. "Now add up those travel points and head for the scorechart at the back of the book to see if you've earned your promotion!"

104. You're in Saudi Arabia, where there's plenty of sand and mirages — illusions created by the heat. That just about describes your hopes of being in the right place. Better head to 18.

105. The taxi driver that you find drives camels instead of cars! You realize that in the deserts of Saudi Arabia, camels must be more reliable than cars. You discuss this and the thief

you're after with the taxi driver.

"Oh, yes," he agrees. "But cars are wonderful. As a matter of fact, the woman you're after loves cars. She said she her next trip would be to a place where they make classic cars."

While you figure out where the chase will take you next, you return to the airport (16).

106. Uganda is famous for its national parks. There are three major ones — the Murchison Falls National Park, the Queen Elizabeth National Park, and the Kidepo Valley National Park.

Among the rare animals that live in these parks are the small forest elephant, both the black and the white rhinoceros, the giraffe, the eland, and the chimpanzee. Among the rarest of these animals is the mountain gorilla, and one has been stolen! It's vital that you find and return it before any harm comes to it.

A local agent arrives to brief you. He's already found three people who saw the thief, and has discovered that only three planes took off before the police sealed the airport.

If you want to talk to:
The cattle herder — go to 77

The banker — go to 95
The travel agent — go to 164

If you're ready to leave for:
The United States of America — go to 29
China — go to 119
Argentina — go to 141

107. You find the chess player waiting for a game. You move your first piece as you sit down. Smiling, the chess player continues the game with you.

"I hear that you saw this woman," you ask, showing him a picture.

"Yes," he agrees. "We played a game together. She was very good, too. She beat me quite quickly. I think you'll have to be as good to find her. Did you know that chess was invented in India in the sixth century and is now played all over the world?"

"Yes," you tell him. "I carry a portable set with me wherever I go. In fact, checkmate."

The player examines the board with astonishment. "Why, you are as good as the woman you seek."

"I try to be," you say, modestly. "Any idea where she might be?"

"I only know that she gave me a generous

tip of twenty American dollars."

You take the hint and match the tip. So she was carrying dollars? You head back to the airport (27).

108. You get off the plane in Buenos Aires, the capital of Argentina. There's an agent from the local office there, but he seems surprised to see you.

"What are you doing here?" he asks. "I'm on the lookout for another agent, not you. I think you'd better head for 18."

109. The pepper picker is working in the fields as you approach her. She's cutting the ripe peppers off the bushes and placing them in a bag.

"I'm looking for a man who stole a famous violin," you tell her. "Do you have any hot tips for me?"

"No," she replies. "But I have plenty of hot peppers."

"Thanks," you say sighing. It's a wasted trip. You head back to the airport (40), hoping for better luck next time.

110. The fish and chip shop is a British tradition, and you see a lot of people buying

fried fish and thick french fries. The shop owner offers you a helping, but you decide to just stick with getting some information.

"I saw the woman you're after," he says. "A lovely blue-eyed lady. She was heading for another country when she stopped in for a helping of fish and chips. Someplace with a lot of rice. Sure you don't want some fish at least?"

You take the hint and buy a large portion. On the way back to the airport (136) you munch it — absolutely delicious!

111. The Maori is a native of New Zealand. He's tall and dignified and greets you with the traditional *hongi*, the rubbing of noses. He's an artist and is carving a piece of wood into the shape of a bird. You ask him about the man you're looking for.

"Yes, I saw that man," he tells you. "He was definitely going to another country, but I don't remember which one. He mentioned something about horse-back riding."

You thank him, leave him to his work, and head back to the airport (42).

112. The samovar salesman is a large man, who greets you with a wide smile. Samovars are large urns that are used for brewing pots of

strong, hot tea. They are made from metal and are highly decorated with figures and artwork. Many of them are so beautiful, they are considered works of art.

"I'm looking for a man with a stolen violin," you tell the salesman.

The man growls. "I remember him," he says. "He tried to steal one of my best samovars! I called the police, but he escaped. If you catch him, punch him in the nose for me!"

"Do you have any idea where he went?" you ask.

"Well, when he ran away, he dropped some money." The samovar salesman shows it to you. It's a ten-rupee note. You thank him and head back to the airport (21).

113. The bonsai bush man is a storekeeper. You stare in amazement at the tiny trees he is growing in elaborate pots. Many of them are less than six inches high, but perfectly formed. "How do you get them to grow this way?" you ask him.

"We use wires to shape the way we want the trees grow," he explains. "We love gardening, but with the land so limited, we developed this art of growing miniature trees to take up less room."

"Well, I'll take up less room by leaving," you

tell him. "Especially if you can give me any information about the man I'm after."

"Is that a gray-eyed thief?" the bush grower asks. "That villain tried to steal a little dogwood that I love. I threw him out and told him to leave the island. He said he was going to go to another island."

You thank him for his help and return to the airport to mull over what he's told you (96).

114. You're on the fabled beaches of Hawaii, watching the surfers. Sadly, not one of them is Ernest Endeavor, and your warrant to arrest him isn't much use here. Better head for 86.

115. Tie your kangaroo down, sport! Here you are in the outback, miles from anywhere, and there's not a sign of the man you've come to arrest, Chuck Roast. You'd better head along to 86 right away.

116. *Mama mia*! You arrive at the opera house just in time for a performance of *The Barber of Seville*. You've obviously had a close shave yourself, because there's no sign at all of Ernest Endeavor in the place. Better head out to 86.

117. You're in the town of Córdoba, Argentina and there's no sign at all of your suspect, Claire

d'Loon. Better go on to 86 to find out what's happened.

118. As you get off the plane in Mecca, you see the pilgrims heading for the sacred sites of the city. They're the only ones here who'll find anything useful, because you're in the wrong spot. You'd better take a flight to 18 right away.

119. You step off the plane in Beijing, China. This is one of the oldest civilized countries in the world. Cities and farms date back six thousand years or more. China was also the first place to invent printing, paper money, pasta, and government-sponsored exams. Hmm, so that's who to blame for all those tests you have take in school.

The local agent arrives with a list. She has found three people who saw the woman you're after, and narrowed down her escape routes to three possible countries.

If you want to speak to:
The librarian — go to 48
The factory worker — go to 9
The weaver — go to 153

If you're ready to leave for:
New Zealand — go to 1

The United Kingdom — go to 87
The United States of America — go to 30

120. You're in Hawaii, one of the world's most popular vacation spots. Unfortunately, you're here for business and not for a vacation. And your business isn't doing too well – you're in the wrong place. Better head off to 18 right away.

121. You get off the plane in Hawaii and look around. There's plenty of sun, sea, and sand, but no local agent. You call the office.

"What are you doing in Hawaii?" the receptionist asks you. "You should be in 18."

122. New York City is home of the New York Stock Exchange, one of the biggest financial organizations in the world. Many of the brokers who work at the exchange have their offices on Wall Street. Your guidebook tells you that a broker is someone who arranges sales for real estate companies or banks. Your contact is a broker, and you find him staring out the window of his big office..

"Yes, I remember the woman you're looking for," he tells you. "She had this idea of making money by cheating people out of stocks. She wanted to pay me in pounds, rather than dollars, but she had a big roll of cash on her. I threw her right out."

You thank him for his help and head back to the airport (63). You're on a roll!

123. You've arrived in Hawaii. It became the fiftieth state of the United States of America in 1959. Hawaii is the name of the main island, but there are over 130 islands in the group. Oahu is the most built-up island, and also home of the famous navy base, Pearl Harbor.

The local agent arrives, almost out of breath. It's a pretty native girl, and she hands you a list.

"That was close," she tells you. "One of the V.I.L.E. agents almost caught me. I've found three people who've seen the thief you're tracking."

"I'll get on it right away," you promise, and look over her information.

If you want to interview:
The used-lei salesman — *go to 33*
The guide at the volcano — *go to 56*
The sailor — *go to 147*

124. Mick from Melbourne turns out to be a sheep shearer. He's busy stripping the ☞

fleece from a sheep when you arrive. He's using what looks like an oversized electric razor. When he sees you, he drops the sheep and lunges for you with the clippers. You quickly throw some cut wool into his face, blinding him. He drops the clippers.

The ranch owner apologizes and calls the police to have Mick picked up. Meanwhile, you head back to the airport (157), certain you're getting very close to solving your case.

125. The fakir is in the marketplace, lying on a bed of sharp nails. And you thought your own bed back home was uncomfortable! It doesn't seem to bother the fakir, though. He tells you he can also walk over hot coals without burning his feet. You hope you never get that cold!

"Maybe you've seen the woman I'm after," you ask him.

"Yes, I have," he answers. "She thought I might teach her some tricks to help her escape from the police. Naturally, I refused to help her."

"Any idea where she disappeared to?" you ask.

"Well, she said something about looking for uranium," the fakir says.

You thank him and head back to the airport (170) to check out what you'll do next.

126. You've arrived in London, one of the busiest cities in the world. Everyone seems to be running about, with plenty to do. The only problem is, there's no local agent here to greet you. You head for the information desk and ask if there are any messages. The desk clerk hands you an envelope with plane tickets inside. Your flight will take you right out to 18.

127. You arrive at the Vatican, which is actually a separate country within the borders of Rome. It's the world's smallest independent country, about one-sixth of a square mile in area, and is ruled by the Pope.

You present the Vatican guards with your warrant to arrest Justin Case, but they tell you he isn't here. Then they order you to report in to 86.

128. Saudi Arabia has large oil fields in the desert, and a lot of people from the United States and England work there. You find the man you're looking for, and he stops his work on the pipelines to talk to you.

"Yes, I recall that man," he tells you. "He

came to me with a silly idea to steal some of the oil from the pipes. I kicked him out. Then he started ranting and raving about tea leaves."

You thank him for his help and head back to the airport (11).

129. Australia has some of the most unusual animals in the world. The animals, which are called marsupials, include kangaroos, wallabies, and the really strange echidna and duck-billed platypus. One thing that isn't here, though, is Luke Warmwater, so your warrant isn't much good. Better head for 86!

130. Italy at last! You're excited to be in this famous country. It has treasures dating back to the Roman Empire. And from the fourteenth through the seventeenth centuries, it was the center of learning for all of Europe. There are many well-known painters and sculptors from that time — Leonardo da Vinci, Michelangelo, Botticelli, and Raphael. There were famous musicians such as Vivaldi and Scarlatti. Galileo also lived during this time; he is best known for his work in astronomy. You realize it must have been an exciting time to live.

Although you wish you could spend days

touring Italy, you're not here to sightsee; it's time to work. The local Acme agent finds you and gives you a list.

"The man you're after was here a short while ago," he tells you. "I've found three people who saw him right after he stole the Stradivarius violin. There are only three flights he could have taken out of the country before I was able to seal off the airport."

You compliment him on his work and study his list.

If you want to interrogate:
The opera singer — *go to 45*
The museum attendant — *go to 137*
The wine presser – *go to 89*

If you're ready to leave for:
Argentina — *go to 108*
The Soviet Union — *go to 21*
New Zealand — *go to 75*

131. You're in China. Just as you step off the plane, you're met by the local Acme agent. "What are you doing here?" he demands to know. "Hurry to 18."

132. The man from Milan has a plan, and he's waiting for your arrival. He's hiding out in

a car factory, waiting to capture you. But you're much smarter than he expected. You sneak in the side door. Using a mirror from one of the cars, you spot where he's lurking behind a car. Then you slip over to the big crane. Using the controls, you silently hook his belt and lift him off the ground.

"Just hanging around as usual?" you ask him as he swings back and forth, yelling curses at you. "Are you going to tell me where the thief is?"

"You'll get nothing out of me!" he howls back at you. As the police take him away, you shudder and think about what nasty plans he probably had for you. Well, never mind, the important thing is that the thief you're after is pretty close! You head back to the airport to try another lead (8).

133. The woman doctor is dressed in a traditional Indian sari, a beautiful flowing and elegant dress, that's formed by winding a long piece of cloth about the body and pinning it into place. In the center of her forehead she has a red spot, which means that she's married.

You ask her about the man you're after, and she nods.

"I saw him," she tells you. "He came to me

74

complaining he had a headache. Apparently, he thought we spoke Spanish in this country!"

You thank her for her help and head back to the airport to check out your options (151).

134. You've arrived at a big cattle ranch in the south of Argentina. There are lots of cattle, and plenty of local gauchos, who are South American cowboys. But there's no sign of Auntie Bellum, so your warrant is useless. It's time to head for 86.

135. When you get off the plane in Saudi Arabia, there's no one to meet you. Checking in at the airline desk, you find a message for you. It's a postcard from China with a message on it:

"Fooled you!"

Curses! You've come to the wrong place. Better head for 18 right away.

136. You're in London, capital of the United Kingdom. It's one of the cultural capitals of the world and has many museums, libraries, and art galleries. There are plenty of historic sights, too, from the Houses of Parliament to Buckingham Palace (where the Queen lives) to St. Paul's Cathedral. A great deal of the city burned down in 1666 A.D., and was rebuilt. Then, during World

War II, it suffered through the Blitz, when the Germans attacked the city, using planes and very early rockets. Since that time, though, it has again been rebuilt.

But you've got very little time to even think about seeing the sights. You're here with a job to do. The local agent arrives, and he's got a list for you.

"Terribly sorry I'm late," he tells you. "The traffic's very bad at this hour, you know." He hands you the list. "But I've narrowed your work down to three people and three possible destinations for you to check out. Ta-ta for now!" With a cheery wave, he sets off again.

If you want to speak to:
The businessman — go to 43
The fish and chip shop owner — go to 110
The bobby — go to 10

If you're ready to leave for:
China — go to 131
The United States — go to 59
India — go to 170

137. The museum contains a large number of famous paintings and several large marble

statues. You find the attendant you're looking for, and ask him why there are so many guards running about the place.

"Because we almost had a painting stolen today," he tells you.

"Sounds like the villain I'm tracking down," you answer. "Can you tell me anything at all about him?"

"Only that he left before taking anything, thank goodness! Now, if you'll excuse me, I'm very busy checking the security systems." He hurries back to his work.

Well, not much help here. You decide to go back to the airport (130) and try another lead.

138. You find the sumo wrestler busy eating in a restaurant. You can't believe the amount of food he has in front of him. You hope you can get him to stop eating for a moment and help you.

"Yes, I saw him," he tells you between mouthfuls. "He had deep gray eyes. And he told me that when he left Japan, he'd be going on to another island."

You thank him for his help and head back to the airport (96).

139. It's bitterly cold when you arrive in Greenland. Soon you realize you're in the

wrong place and your spirit sinks even lower than the temperature. You sigh and head off for 18.

140. You're in Hawaii, and armed with a warrant to arrest Claire d'Loon. It's a pity she isn't here. Better move on to 86.

141. Argentina is a large country, taking up most of the southern part of South America. But you've looked through the entire country and the person you're tracking isn't here. Better head to 18 right now.

142. Your plane lands in Buenos Aires, Argentina. You read that Buenos Aires was founded in 1536 and stands on the banks of the river Plate. It's a center of learning, with several universities and an opera house of its own. It's also the home of the world's largest Spanish-language publisher. You wish you could speak Spanish right now.

The local agent arrives with a list for you. Thankfully, it's in English!

"I've been very thorough in checking," the agent tells you. "There are three people who have seen the person you are after. And there's no sign that he's left the country yet."

"Then I'd better act fast," you answer, studying his list.

If you want to speak to:

The book publisher — go to 156

The bank teller — go to 69

The university professor — go to 149

143. The fisherman doesn't seem to be having any luck, but you hope you'll do better. Maybe he can help you catch something — like the thief you're after!

"Yes. I've seen this man. His hair is brown."

"Any idea where he's heading?" you ask.

"Well, he mentioned something about buying dates," the fisherman answers. Right then, he gets a bite on his line. Leaving him to reel in his fish, you head back to the airport (68) real fast.

144. You step off the plane in San Juan, Puerto Rico. An agent from the local office spots you and comes over. He gives you new plane tickets.

"I was told you were on your way," he says. "But you're to go directly to 18."

145. This is Ottawa, capital of Canada. Canada is an old country, probably first discovered by Viking explorers from Iceland in

the eleventh century. The French colonized it in the seventeenth century and called it New France, but the British won the whole country in the eighteenth century. Quebec, one of the provinces of Canada, still remains mostly French and is legally recognized as a "distinct society" from the rest of Canada.

When the agent from the local office arrives, and has some good news for you. "There are three people who've spotted the woman you're after, and three possible flights she could have taken out of the country."

If you want to question:
The lumberjack — go to 37
Yukon Tom — go to 97
The Mountie — go to 150

If you're ready to leave for:
Saudi Arabia — go to 16
The United States of America — go to 49
The United Kingdom — go to 126

146. You've ended up in Walla Walla, out in the Australian desert. But as the Aussies say, you're up a gum tree, because Ernest Endeavor, the man you've got a warrant for, isn't here. You'd better head for 86 on the double.

147. You find the sailor at Pearl Harbor naval base. It's a very large place, filled with people working away on the ships. However, the sailor you find is a V.I.L.E. henchman who tries to throw you off the dock.

You struggle together, but he goes overboard instead, when you do a clever judo toss. The local Military Police fish him out and take him off to a cell to dry out.

Head back to the airport because you're getting very close (123)!

148. The pretzel seller has a stall on Fifth Avenue, one of the busiest streets in all of New York City. He sells huge pretzels that are over six inches wide, and piping hot. It's lunchtime, and busy office workers line up at his cart to buy pretzels. You ask the seller about the man

you're after.

"Yes, I've seen this man," he tells you. "He stopped by to stock up on pretzels. He told me that where he's going they eat a lot of fish, and he never touches the stuff."

You thank him and hurry back to the airport (74).

149. When you arrive at the university, there's a professor waiting for you.

"I'll teach you to mind your own business!" she yells, and tries to push you out the classroom window. You sidestep quickly, trip her, but manage to grab her before she falls over the edge.

"Pig!" she yells. "You'll learn nothing from me!" You realize she's not a professor at all, but a V.I.L.E. henchman.

The police arrive and take her away. You head back to the airport (142). You must be really hot on the trail!

150. The Mountie is a Canadian mounted policeman. They are legendary for tracking a crook thousands of miles if they have to. They certainly earned the reputation that, "a Mountie always gets his man."

You ask him about the woman you're after.

"Yes, I recall her well," he tells you. "She had hair almost as red as my coat! Pity I didn't know she was a criminal I could have arrested her for you."

You agree it's a shame and head back for the airport (145).

151. Your plane has landed in New Delhi, India. India is a large country, bounded on the north by the Himalayan Mountains. There are a large number of rivers in the country, the most famous of which is the Ganges. The two important religions of Buddhism and Hinduism both began here. It is also one of the most densely populated countries in the world.

India was made up of a lot of small, independent states until it was colonized by England during the 1800's. In 1947 India became independent once again.

When you land at the airport, you struggle through the crowd to reach the local Acme agent . Finally he's able to hand you a list.

"I've contacted three people who saw the person you're after, and there are three places he might have gone from here."

If you want to talk to:
The snake charmer — go to 34

The Sikh — go to 19
The doctor — go to 133

If you want to head for:
Argentina — go to 90
Puerto Rico — go to 40
Japan — go to 62

152. You're in Puerto Rico, a small island in the Caribbean. There's no one here to meet you, so you phone the local office.

"Aren't you supposed to be in 18?" the receptionist asks.

Uh-oh! You hang up and head to 18 fast.

153. Woven baskets have been used in China for thousands of years. Basket weaving is still considered a valued skill. When you spot the basket weaver at her market stall, you're amazed at how fast and skillfully her fingers move.

"Have you seen the woman I'm looking for?" you ask, showing her a picture.

"She was here a short while ago and said that she was leaving for another country and needed to change her money into dollars."

You thank her and head back to the airport (119), making a note to remember to change your own money into dollars as well!

154. The plane touches down in Italy. You head for the information desk. "Anyone been asking for me?"

"Here's a postcard for you," says the desk clerk. You see that it's a picture of the Great Wall of China. On the back is a short poem:

Roses are red,
Violets are blue,
You're in the wrong place —
So phooey to you!"

You sigh with disgust. Tricked! Better head for 18.

155. Your plane lands in Honshu, Japan, but there's no one to greet you. Knowing how polite the Japanese are, this puzzles you. Then you discover that you're in the wrong place! You should move on to 18.

156. The publishing house is a big, empty building. Fortunately, the only person you see is the man you're looking for. When he sees you, he tries to topple a pile of boxes filled with books onto you. You jump out of the way just in time to avoid being pressed flat. The V.I.L.E. henchman tries to run, but you pick up one of

the fallen books and hit him over the head with it. He collapses.

While you wait for the police to arrive, you search through his pockets. You find a little black book. Inside it are written the names and addresses of all the possible suspects in this case! The break you've been waiting for!

The police arrive and take away the unconscious man. You go back to examining your list. If you want to go after:

Carmen Sandiego — go to 31
"Auntie" Bellum — go to 134
Ernest Endeavor — go to 55
Chuck Roast — go to 103
Kari Meback — go to 167
Claire d'Loon — go to 117
Justin Case — go to 93
Luke Warmwater — go to 72

157. You've arrived in Canberra, Australia. Australia is an island so huge that it forms a continent all by itself. It also contains some of the most unusual animals in the world. Among these strange creatures that live on an island off the southern coast are the wombat, the koala bear, (not really a bear, though often called one); and the ferocious Tasmanian devil, (which is really a just meat-eating mammal

that looks like a large dog).

And off the eastern coast stretches the Great Barrier Reef. You read in your guidebook that a reef is a rocky shelf near the shores of great bodies of water. You also read that the Great Barrier Reef is actually a whole host of small reefs in a line almost 1,250 miles long! Too bad you can't take some time off to study the local wildlife.

You look around for the local agent, but he's nowhere to be seen. That's odd. Then you hear a noise from a broom closet. When you open the door, you find the agent tied up and gagged. Quickly you free him.

"Thank goodness you've arrived!" he gasps. "I think you're on to something! I spoke to three people who've seen the crook you're after. One of them must have knocked me out and stuck me in here to keep me from talking to you. Good thing you heard me."

You agree, and study the list of contacts that he hands you.

If you want to interrogate:

The kangaroo wrangler — *go to 3*

Mick from Melbourne — *go to 124*

Crocodile Humphrey — *go to 70*

158. You're in Pompeii, on the slopes of Mount Vesuvius, looking for Chuck Roast, and

you're armed with a warrant. Unfortunately, you have no luck finding Chuck. Head for 86.

159. You've landed in Italy, one of the most artistic countries in the world. There are plenty of painters, singers, and sculptors, but no contacts for you. Someone has artfully misled you. Better head for 18.

160. Your plane touches down in the United Kingdom. It's very foggy, and a lot of the fog is inside your head. You're in the wrong place. Get back on a plane and go to 18.

161. You find the taxi driver you're looking for, uptown at the Cloisters in Fort Tryon Park. The Cloisters is one of your favorite spots in New York City. It's a museum made up of parts of monasteries and churches shipped over from Europe. It's always peaceful here, no matter how wild the rest of New York might be.

"So," the driver asks as you get in, "you after anything special?"

"I'm after the man who stole the torch from the Statue of Liberty," you tell him.

"Yeah, I heard about that robbery. You know, I picked up a guy who wanted to get to the airport — fast. Said he was heading off to a place where they spend krones. Hey, where do you want to go?"

"The airport — fast," you tell him. What luck to get such a hot lead just as you head out (74).

162. You find the sitar player. The sitar looks like a guitar with a long neck and seven strings. When the sitar player stops, you talk to him about the woman you're looking for.

"Yes, I remember her," he says. "She said she loves music played on string instruments. She also said she was going where they play the Spanish guitar."

You thank him for the information and music and head back to the airport (170).

163. You're in Hawaii, where some of the most beautiful orchids in the world are grown. You know that Auntie Bellum has a passion for orchids, and you've got a warrant for her arrest. But though you find plenty of orchids, there's no sign of Auntie Bellum. You eventually pack it in and head for 86.

164. The travel agent you visit is a cheerful man, who tries to sell you seventeen different package tours — from going over Niagara Falls

in a barrel to climbing Mount Everest. You finally manage to tell him that you're just here on business, tracking down a stolen gorilla.

"Yes, I remember that lady," he tells you. "She said she was going to look for some marble when she left here."

You thank him for his help and leave before he offers to book you on a flight to the moon! You go straight to the airport (106).

165. You're in the outback, mate. That's right — the middle of the desert. There's nothing to be seen for miles around, especially Carmen Sandiego. Your warrant won't do you much good here. You'd better go to 86 instead.

166. The fisherman is the only person you've seen along the banks of the river. Despite the number of fish here in Argentina, fishing is not popular, and most people don't eat fish. You can't think why — personally, you love a good piece of catfish!

You ask the man about the woman you're looking for. He smiles.

"Ah, she was a beauty, that one!" he replies. "I wanted to go with her, but she said she was off to change her money into American dollars."

You thank him and wish him luck with his

fishing. You're off to try and catch a big fish of your own! It's back to the airport (52)!

167. Well, you're out on the pampas of Argentina and also out of luck. There's no sign of Kari Meback. Your warrant won't do you a lot of good here. Time to go to 86.

168. You've arrived back in the United States of America, and run right into trouble. There's a message for you from the Chief that tells you to head straight to 18, or you're fired!

169. When you find the librarian she greets you with a bright smile. When she asks what you're looking for, you tell her that you're after a woman with a stolen gorilla.

"I think the person you're after was here. She was looking up books on timber."

"Maybe she was trying to build a cage for the gorilla," you suggest. Thanking her for her help, you head back to the airport (1).

170. You've arrived in India. You wish that you had time to see the famous Taj Mahal, or the wildlife of India — the Indian elephant, the rhinoceros, or the magnificent tigers.

But duty calls. With a sigh, you find the

local Acme agent. He hands you a list. There are three people who've seen the woman you're tracking, and only three places that she could have gone to.

If you want to interview:
The sitar player — go to 162
The police officer — go to 4
The fakir — go to 125

If you're ready to leave for:
Argentina — go to 52
Saudi Arabia — go to 104
Puerto Rico — go to 25

SCORE CHART

Add up your travel points (you remembered to mark one down each time you moved to a new number, didn't you?). If you had to add on penalty points for trying to arrest the wrong person, do that as well. Then check your score against the chart below to see how you did.

0 – 17: You really didn't do it in this few steps, did you? Either you're boasting about your abilities, or you're actually working with Carmen's gang. Be honest, and try again. If you dare!

18 – 40: Super-sleuth! You work very well and don't waste time. Well done — you deserve the new rank and the nice big bonus you'll get next payday!

41 – 60: Private-eye material! You're a good, steady worker, and you get your man (or woman). Still, there's room for improvement, and you can always try again to get another promotion.

61 – 80: Detective first class. You're not quite a world-famous private eye yet, but you'll get there. Try again, and see if you can't make it up a grade or two!

81 – 100: Rookie material. You're taking too long to track down these crooks. Next time, they're going to get away from you. You'd better study a little harder and try again. You really are better than this!

Over 100: Are you sure you're really cut out to be a detective? Maybe you'd be better off looking for an easier job — a shoe salesman, perhaps? But if you're determined to be a detective, why not try again. Maybe this was just an off day? Better luck next time!